Calling the Wind

A STORY OF
HEALING AND HOPE

Trudy Ludwig & Kathryn Otoshi

Alfred A. Knopf   New York

fuyu (winter)

a family's loss
fills every room with silence
words freeze, unspoken

Memories rush in.

Feelings too big to hold inside must find a way out.

"Moshi moshi? (Hello?)

Are you there? It's me.

Can you hear me?

I just hear the wind. Is that you?"

"I feel like you're here, somewhere."

"Moshi moshi?

It's not fair!

Why did it have to be you?"

"Mama—where are you?

Are any puppies there with you?

Please come home."

"Moshi moshi?

If only you . . .

If only I . . .

If only."

"Yellow was her favorite color."

"It's not the same without you.

We're not the same without you.

I miss you. We all do."

haru (spring)

pain's sharp edge softens
heavy hearts become lighter
hope blossoms anew

"I made a new friend in my class.
Her name is Natsuki—same as yours!"

". . . and I will always hold you
in my heart."

"Guess what? I just got on the
baseball team! I play first base!"

"I still see you as a
little girl, folding all
those paper cranes."

"Can you tell
Dad to get us
a puppy?"

Even when a life ends, love lives on.

"Ah . . . how your mom loved paper cranes."

"She would have loved a puppy, too. Can we get one?"

For the Ludwig, Long,
and Roseman families
—T.L.

For the Malabuyo family
and the Grant Imahara
STEAM Foundation
—K.O.

Matthew Komatsu

The Wind Phone (Kaze no Denwa)

Calling the Wind is a work of fiction inspired by kaze no denwa, the wind phone created by Itaru Sasaki of Ōtsuchi, Japan. In 2010, Sasaki set up in his backyard garden a glass-paned phone booth to house an old rotary telephone. The phone wasn't connected to anything, but that didn't matter to Sasaki. He just needed a quiet and safe space to voice his grief over the death of his beloved cousin.

After the earthquake and tsunami hit Japan in 2011, word got out about Sasaki's wind phone. People who were grieving over the loss of loved ones from these natural disasters soon started showing up in his backyard, wanting to use the phone, too. And he kindly let them. Over the years, many people from numerous countries have gone there to find peace. To this day, the phone booth sits on that little windy hill overlooking the Pacific Ocean and waits for the next caller.

Recommended Resources on Grief

Coalition to Support Grieving Students (grievingstudents.org)

Dougy Center, The National Grief Center for Children & Families (dougy.org)

National Alliance for Children's Grief (childrengrieve.org)

*"My thoughts could not be relayed
over a regular phone line.
I wanted them to be carried on the
wind. It's a way to stay in touch,
to let them know that they're still
a big part of our family."*
—Itaru Sasaki

THIS IS A BORZOI BOOK PUBLISHED BY ALFRED A. KNOPF

Text copyright © 2022 by Trudy Ludwig
Jacket art and interior illustrations copyright © 2022 by Kathryn Otoshi
All rights reserved. Published in the United States by Alfred A. Knopf,
an imprint of Random House Children's Books, a division of Penguin Random House LLC, New York.
Knopf, Borzoi Books, and the colophon are registered trademarks of Penguin Random House LLC.

Visit us on the Web! rhcbooks.com
Educators and librarians, for a variety of teaching tools, visit us at RHTeachersLibrarians.com

Library of Congress Cataloging-in-Publication Data
Names: Ludwig, Trudy, author. | Otoshi, Kathryn, illustrator.
Title: Calling the wind: a story of healing and hope / Trudy Ludwig; [illustrated by] Kathryn Otoshi.
Description: First edition. | New York: Alfred A. Knopf, 2022. | Audience: Ages 4–8. |
Summary: A Japanese family mourns the loss of a wife and mother by making origami cranes and using the Wind
Telephone to communicate their feelings of loss and yearning. Identifiers: LCCN 2021039416 (print) | LCCN 2021039417 (ebook)
| ISBN 978-0-593-42640-1 (hardcover) | ISBN 978-0-593-42641-8 (library binding) | ISBN 978-0-593-42642-5 (ebook)
Subjects: LCSH: Bereavement—Juvenile fiction. | Grief—Juvenile fiction. | Mothers—Juvenile fiction. | Families—Japan—Juvenile fiction. |
Winds—Juvenile fiction. | Japan—Social life and customs—Juvenile fiction. | CYAC: Grief—Fiction. | Mothers—Fiction. | Family life—Japan—
Fiction. | Winds—Fiction. | Japan—Fiction. Classification: LCC PZ7.L9763 Cal 2022 (print) | LCC PZ7.L9763 (ebook) | DDC [E]—dc23
The illustrations were created using Kuretake watercolors, colored pencils, and pens.
Book design by Sarah Hokanson
MANUFACTURED IN CHINA 10 9 8 7 6 5 4 3 2 1 First Edition